Baxter Bear
and
Moses Moose

Baxter Bear and Moses Moose

By Evariste Bernier
Illustrated by Dawn Peterson

Down East Books

ISBN 0-89272-287-8 (hardcover)
ISBN 0-89272-413-7 (softcover)
Library of Congress Catalog Card Number 90-61408

2 4 6 8 9 7 5 3

Printed and bound in Hong Kong through Four Colour Imports

Down East Books
Camden, Maine 04843

For Lynn

Baxter Bear didn't have any friends, because he was different. He never fished for his dinner in the stream the way the other bears did. He did not forage for blueberries or raspberries in the fields. He would not even climb a tree for honey. And Baxter had a very unusual hobby for a black bear from Maine: he collected hats.

He had blue hats and black hats, brown hats, and beige hats. He had purple hats, polka-dotted, and paisley.

He had gray hats, green hats, gold hats, and gaudy hats. He had tall hats and short hats, hard hats and soft hats. He had smart hats and dumb hats. He had sun hats and rain hats; he even had snow hats.

Often Baxter got his new hats through the mail by ordering them over the telephone. Sometimes he could find a hat or two at a campsite that had been left behind by some hikers. And sometimes he would get out his needle and thread to make a new hat from scratch.

Baxter Bear had plenty of hats, but what he didn't have was enough space to keep them all.

"My drawers are full of hats. My closet is full of hats. I have hats in the basement. I have hats in the attic. Even my refrigerator is bursting with hats."

He thought, "Maybe I ought to give away some of my hats." But he shook his head sadly. "Since I don't have any friends, I couldn't even give away a hat, could I?"

Baxter scratched his head. "What I need is a really big hat rack. Let's see . . . what would make a good hat rack? A broom? Rabbit ears from the TV? A chair?

"How about some moose antlers? If I got a really big pair, I could hang up lots of hats. But first I'll have to find a moose who'd be willing to give me his antlers. Maybe I have something for which a moose would want to trade."

Baxter Bear opened his closet door and dug down to the bottom of a pile of hats. "Here's my old toaster. This might be good for trading—everyone likes toast. I can take it into the woods and make some cinnamon toast. A hungry moose will come running just as soon as he smells the delicious food. I'll tell him that he can have all the toast he can eat, but first he has to give me his antlers."

Then he took a closer look at the toaster. "Wait a minute! I can't make cinnamon toast in the forest: there's no place in the woods to plug in a toaster. Boy, what a silly idea that was!"

Baxter put the toaster back where he had found it and pulled out a pumpkin. "Hey, this might be good for trading! A moose will come along, see this pumpkin, and ask if he can have it to carve for Halloween. I'll tell him that, sure, he can have the pumpkin, but only if he gives me his antlers."

Baxter lugged the pumpkin out of the closet, but then he thought of something. "Today isn't Halloween. A moose isn't going to want to make a jack-o-lantern if it isn't Halloween. Moose are like that—never thinking about the future. My goodness, moose are silly, aren't they?"

He put the pumpkin back under the pile of hats. "Shucks, I thought I'd found something really good to trade that time. But there must be something around here a moose would like."

Then Baxter pulled out a long wooden back scratcher. "I thought I'd lost this," he said as he began to scratch his back in all the hard-to-reach places. "Boy, that feels good! Moose are lucky: they have antlers they can use to scratch an itch. It's like having a built-in back scratcher—except in the winter, that is. Moose shed their antlers every winter so they can grow brand-new ones in the spring."

Baxter Bear took a good look at the back scratcher and almost shouted. "That's it! I'll trade this back scratcher for the antlers. What moose wouldn't just love to have a back scratcher after he'd lost his?

BAXTER
BEAR

"But before I go looking for a moose I'd better pack some provisions. One never knows when one may need more hats. It could rain or something, or possibly even snow. That's the way it is with the weather up here in Maine. And what if there were a total eclipse of the sun? I wouldn't want to be caught without my coal miner's hat."

Soon Baxter Bear's knapsack was bulging with hats. "Here I go," he said. "Off to the woods to find a moose. I'll trade him this nifty back scratcher for a moose-antler hat rack. Then I'll have room for lots more hats."

Just as Baxter Bear was beginning his search for a moose, in the very same forest, a moose was working on a problem of his own. Moses Moose had cold feet, and since moose have such very large feet, this was a particularly big problem for him.

Moses had tried just about everything to warm up his feet. He had tried standing on hot water bottles, but he was too heavy and they broke.

He had tried wrapping himself up in an electric blanket, but he was kind of clumsy. No matter how hard he tried, one foot always seemed to stick out.

He had even tried putting his hooves up two at a time on the stove hearth; that only made his other feet feel even colder.

But Moses did not like to give up on a problem until he had solved it. After a great deal of thought, he believed that he had finally come up with a solution.

"It's actually quite simple," he said. "Why didn't I think of it before? All I have to do is put something warm down on my floor—some kind of rug. That would keep my feet off the cold floor.

"But what kind of rug should I get? It has to be something large and thick and very warm. And I would like it to look good too.

"I know—how about a bearskin rug? That would do just fine. Bears are big and they have very thick fur. And a bear-skin rug would look lovely in front of my fireplace.

"But how do I get a bearskin rug? I wouldn't want to have to harm the poor creature. Let's see, don't bears hibernate in winter? And isn't that when I'll need the rug? Maybe I could get a bear to fall asleep in my living room. If I had a friend who was a bear, I could just invite him over and wait for him to fall asleep." Moses shook his head sadly. "But I don't have any friends at all. I guess I'll just have to catch a bear and bring him here.

"I'll need something to help me catch him. I'll have to set up a trap." Moses went to his closet and took out some rope. "I can tie this rope into a lasso and lay it on the ground. Then, when a bear steps into it, I'll pull on the rope and tie him up."

ALDER
BARK BITS

"Now all I have to do is think of a way to get a bear to step into the middle of the lasso. I have to put something there to attract him—maybe a present, something a bear would especially like."

Moses went back to the closet. "There must be something in here I could give a bear." He pulled out a painting of two moose ballet dancing. "This is a pretty picture. But I bet a bear would not be interested in a painting of moose. If there were two bears ballet dancing in the picture, that would be different, but I don't have any pictures of bears.

"There must be something else in here that a bear would like." Moses took out a plastic pink flamingo. "This might be good. Everybody likes pink flamingos. Oh, wait—I always put this on my lawn in the summer. I guess I should keep it."

Next, he took out a jar that had the word HONEY written on it. "Here's something I know bears like—honey." He looked inside the jar. "But there's no honey in here. An empty honey jar wouldn't be a very good present for a bear, now would it?"

Moses looked inside the honey jar again. "Of course! I could still give this jar to a bear and just tell him I'll put some honey in it later."

Then Moses had what he thought was a brilliant idea. "I'll put in an IOU for the honey." He went to his writing desk and took out a piece of paper and a pen. Very carefully he wrote down the message: "Dear Mr. Bear, this is an I-OWE-YOU for the honey that goes inside this jar." He signed the note and held it up to admire.

He folded the piece of paper and put the IOU inside the honey jar. Then he placed the jar into a box, wrapped the package in colored paper, and put a big bow on top.

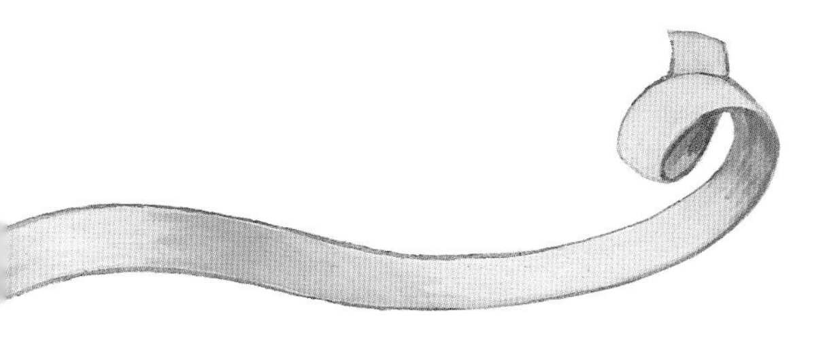

"There. I have the perfect present for a bear. After he sees this pretty wrapping paper, he will walk right into the middle of the lasso to open his gift. That's when I'll pull on the rope and catch him. I'll tie him up and bring him to my house, and after he falls asleep for the winter, he will be my bearskin rug. This winter I'm not going to have cold feet at all."

Moses picked up the rope and the gift. He went out the door and headed off into the woods to set a trap for a bear.

MOSES MOOSE

While Moses Moose was looking for just the right spot to set a bear trap, Baxter Bear was walking along calling for a moose.

"Here moosie. Here, moosie, moosie, moosie," he called.

"Gee," he said. "The moose I'm looking for must not be very smart. He doesn't come when I call. There must be another way I can find a moose."

Just then Baxter heard a snapping sound. He stopped in his tracks and looked all around, but he didn't see anyone. Then he looked down at his feet and saw that he was standing on a small broken branch. "That was just me stepping on a twig."

He bent down to look more closely at the twig. When he moved his foot he saw that he'd left a paw print on the ground. Baxter looked back to where he'd been walking and saw the long line of prints he'd left behind. "That's it!" he shouted. "If I can find some moose tracks they will surely lead me to a moose."

Baxter walked along carefully, looking for moose tracks. Every now and then he straightened up again to call, "Here moosie, moosie, moosie."

And while Baxter Bear walked along, calling for moose and looking for tracks, Moses Moose patiently waited for a bear to step into his trap. He had placed the lasso on the ground and he had put the bear's beautifully wrapped present in the middle. Then Moses went to stand behind a big tree to wait for a bear to come along and find the present.

"I hope this doesn't take too long. I hope it doesn't start to rain or snow—that would be even worse. Then my feet would really get cold." Moses shivered just thinking about it.

"What was that? I thought I heard someone—maybe it's a bear. Oh, please be a bear! I hope he likes the empty jar of honey and the IOU I have for him."

"Here moosie, moosie, moosie," Baxter called.

Just then Moses saw Baxter Bear. And just as Moses saw Baxter, Baxter saw Moses Moose.

"It's a moose," shouted Baxter. "Look at those beautiful antlers! They will make a perfect hat rack."

And Moses cried, "It's a bear! He'll make a beautiful bearskin rug."

Baxter raised the long wooden back scratcher to show Moses what he had brought to trade.

"Eeeek!" Moses shouted. "What's that?"

"It's a back scratcher," Baxter explained. "I brought it to trade with you. How else am I going to get a hat rack?"

"What hat rack?" Moses asked. "What are you talking

about? Wouldn't you like to open the present I brought you?"

"A present for me? Why, thank you." Baxter Bear put down the back scratcher and walked toward the colorful package.

"Just stand in the middle of the lasso," Moses said. "Then you can pick up your present. I hope you like it."

As Baxter Bear stepped into the middle of the lasso and lifted his present, Moses pulled on the rope. The lasso tightened around Baxter's leg. High into the air he flew, still holding the package. He was so excited about opening the present that he didn't even notice he was now upside-down.

"Gee," he said. "No one ever gave me a present before. This is a very pretty jar. I like the way the word HONEY is written on the outside."

"I'm sorry there isn't any honey on the inside," Moses told him.

Baxter looked into the jar. "Yes, I guess you are right. It does seem to be empty."

"That's what the note is for," Moses explained. "It's an IOU for the honey. It says that someday I'll give you the honey that goes in the jar."

"Oh, that's OK," Baxter said. "I like the jar just the way it is. I don't like honey anyway—it gives me the hiccups. I can put the note up on my wall. It's the first note I have ever gotten from a moose and it's really quite handsome. Did you write it?"

"Yes, I did," Moses said proudly.

Baxter looked at the jar again. "Did I tell you how much I like this jar? I could keep a hat in it. Maybe two if they were small. Speaking of hats, Mr. Moose . . ."

"Oh, please, Mr. Bear, call me Moses. That's what all my friends call me. Well, actually, I mean that if I had any friends, they would want to call me Moses because that's my name."

"And you may call me Baxter. My name is Baxter Bear because that's what it says on my mailbox."

"I am very pleased to meet you, Baxter."

Baxter looked around. "Moses, this may sound strange, but I seem to be upside-down."

"I know," Moses said. "That's because you are hanging from this rope that I am holding with my foot."

"Oh. In that case, would you mind letting me down? All the ideas in my head are bumping into each other."

Moses shook his head. "I'm sorry, but I don't think I can do that. You see, I have been waiting some time for a bear just like you to come along. I have cold feet, so I need a bearskin rug. A rug will help to keep them warm."

"That's a shame about your cold feet," Baxter said. "You know, I have been looking for a moose."

"Why do you want a moose?" Moses asked.

"Because I collect hats and I need a moose-antler hat rack. I see that you have a wonderful rack of antlers there, Moses. I could hang lots of hats from a hat rack like that."

"Oh, would you like these? I'd be happy to give them to you just as soon as I'm done with them."

"You would? Why thank you," Baxter said. "That would be just wonderful. That's why I brought along this back scratcher—I was going to trade it for your antlers."

"Oh, you don't need to trade me anything," Moses said. "I don't have much use for my antlers after I've shed them. In fact, I'll be happy to give you a pair every year so you can collect lots more hats. So, will you come and sleep on my living room floor each winter?"

HONEY

Baxter shook his head. "Bears like to spend the winter in cozy, dark dens. I could not fall asleep on a hard floor. I was just thinking about your cold feet, though, and I had an idea.

"I have all kinds of hats. Some of them are made of wool and are very warm," Baxter explained. "We can take apart some hats and sew the pieces together to make you socks and slippers. That will help to keep your feet warm."

"That's a *great* idea," Moses exclaimed. "You are a bear just full of good ideas."

"How kind of you to say that!" Baxter said. "No one has ever said that about me before. Maybe it's just easier for me to think upside-down."

"Oh, I almost forgot." Moses let Baxter down from the tree very gently.

"Thank you," Baxter Bear said.

"You're welcome," said Moses Moose.

From that day on, Baxter got all the hat racks he could use and Moses never had cold feet again. And both of them had something much more valuable than just hat racks or slippers and socks—they each had a friend.

The End

ABOUT THE ARTIST

Dawn Peterson lives in Camden, Maine, where she is a freelance graphic designer and illustrator. Her work has been published in several magazines of regional and outdoor interest, and this is her first children's book. She has had occasional encounters with moose near her home, but—as yet—not one bear.